In honor of all who have served, sacrificed, and given their lives for the United States of America.

History Among Us - A Collection of Short Stories from the Civil War

Written by Priscilla Kis

Cover Photo by Marrius Kis

Illustrations by Elissa Kis

Table of Contents

Part 1: In the Confederate Camp

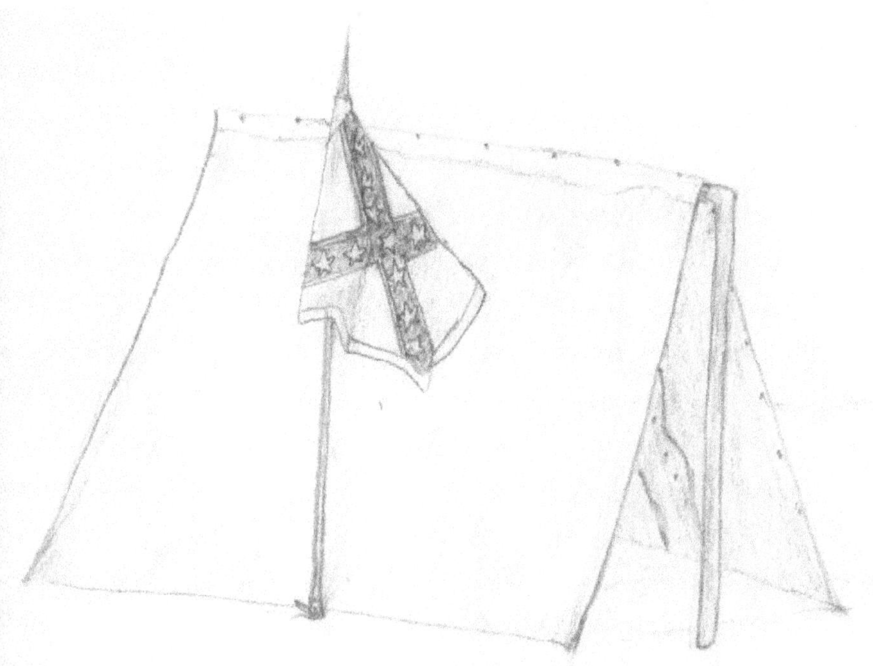

1. A Coat for One With None

Daniel, a young 16 year old courier for the Confederate army, leaned forward on his horse and urged it to go faster. The wind whipped around his ragged uniform and the rain fell in torrents. He huddled over, willing the horse to arrive sooner at their destination.

As darkness fell, he spotted a light in a window in the distance. He squinted towards the building to determine if he arrived. "Yep. Let's go to the stables, boy, then I'll go in." He said to the horse as he patted its mane. He pulled up by the home and shakily dismounted. He then took the reins in his shivering hands and led the horse to the stables.

The inside smelled like sweet hay, and the courier stood in the entrance for a bit, breathing deeply. "Nothin' better than that smell." His horse nudged his shoulder. "I know ol' boy, you'd rather eat it!" He grinned as he led the horse to a stall.

He spent several moments blowing vigorously over his hands to warm them up. He then picked up some hay and dropped it in front of the horse. He grabbed a bucket, braced himself, and stepped outside in the storm to go get water.

With his horse watered and fed, Daniel was ready to enter the home. He left the stable once again towards the building. The wind ruffled his hair, and the rain pounded on him. Exposure to this cold weather all day made him start shivering uncontrollably. He stepped up to the building's door, knocked, and waited.

"Yes?" A guard looked out.

"Sir, I h-h-have a m-message for General Lee." Daniel said through chattering teeth.

The door swung wide open. "He's in that room." The guard pointed.

"Thank you sir." The boy said as he entered the warm building. He walked up to the room and knocked.

The door opened, and General Lee looked out. "Why come in my boy," He said with surprise. "I didn't think you'd come on this terrible day!"

Daniel smiled. "An-nything for you, s-sir," he said, trying to not slur his words from the cold. He reached into his pocket and pulled out the message he came to deliver. "For you." He handed it to the General.

"Thank you, Son. Come, sit by the fire," General Lee said while pulling up a chair beside him.

Daniel gratefully sat down, "Thank you sir." He was suddenly aware of his shabby appearance. He leaned forward by the fire and ducked his head, trying to hide his threadbare clothes.

General Lee sat silently and opened the message, while observing Daniel out of the corner of his eyes. "Some storm you rode through. Thank you for delivering this message."

Daniel shyly glanced up at the General, "You're welcome, Sir."

"Have you eaten yet?" General Lee asked.

"Yes sir, right before heading out here."

"Would you like more?"

Daniel shook his head, "Thank you sir, but I'm alright." He said as he put his hands closer by the fire.

Several minutes later, after thoroughly warming himself, Daniel slowly rose. "Thank you, General, for your hospitality." He said with a salute.

General Lee looked at him intently, "Are you returning at once to your commander?"

"Yes, sir, if my horse has finished feeding."

General Lee looked outside. "It is still raining very hard, you don't have a rubber coat?"

"Oh, that don't matter, General," the boy bravely replied.

General Lee stood silently for a moment. Then he turned, walked to where his rubber coat was hanging, took it down, and gave it to the unsuspecting soldier.

"No, sir, General, I can't take this and deprive you of it!" Daniel protested as he held it out to Lee.

"No, you need it more than me." The General said with a smile.

"I....General, thank you." Daniel stammered..

General Lee smiled, "I hope we meet again. Take care of yourself, Son."

"Thank you sir, I will." Daniel said while smartly saluting his General.

Lee smiled and returned the salute. Then the boy turned around and left the room. He walked out the building to get his horse.

I will never forget this day. He thought with gratitude.

2. Lee's Consideration for His Men

Private Theodore Hartman of the 14th Tennessee Infantry dragged his feet along the road. His regiment had been marching for several days with little rest and nourishment.

"You suppose we're anywhere near stopping?" A young soldier to Theodore's right panted.

Theodore looked at him and sighed, "Who knows, Andrew. I reckon we will soon. When this old war is over we'll surely be able to rest!"

The tired regiment continued trudging, footsore and exhausted. Eventually, they reached a narrower portion of road in the woods. The soldiers slowed down and hesitated, before their colonel came up. "Alright boys, we can rest awhile here."

The group of tired soldiers instantly sat down. Theodore quickly lay down on the dirt road, using his knapsack as a pillow.

Andrew plopped down next to him. "Whew, I thought we'd never stop!"

Theodore nodded, while looking around. Some soldiers were lying down with their eyes shut. One was cleaning his musket. Another was rubbing his sore feet. And another had pulled out some hardtack to eat while resting. Theodore closed his eyes and basked in the comfortable autumn air. The trees up in Northern Virginia had burst into hues of red and orange, and the crisp fall air filled the soldiers' lungs. He sighed contentedly.

After about ten minutes of quietly lying on the ground, Theodore heard the clopping of horse hooves down the road. He raised himself on his elbow for a better look. Five officers on horses, including General Hill and General Lee, were approaching them.

General Hill rode several feet ahead of the rest of the officers and came up by Theodore. "Move out the road, men," he ordered.

Before any soldier could move, General Lee spoke up. "Never mind, General; we will ride around them. Lie still, men." While speaking Lee turned his horse over to the left and passed the resting men on the side of the road. General Hill turned bright red with shame and he, along with the rest of the officers, were quick to follow.

The soldiers quietly looked on until all officers had passed. After several moments of silence, Theodore spoke up. "I never saw such a thing in all my life."

The rest of the men heartily agreed. They all strained their eyes to see their General one last time as he rode off in the distance.

3. Lee and the Hungry Soldier

Henry Smith wearily trudged down the muddy road. He shifted his rifle with difficulty, and concentrated on putting one foot in front of the other. His stomach rumbled, but he tried to ignore it. As he avoided the puddles scattered along the road, he noticed a tent nearby with an older man standing in the entrance looking out at Henry's regiment as it marched by.

Henry walked up to the tent. "Hello! Got anything to eat in there?" He called.

The older gentleman looked at Henry kindly, "Yes, what's the matter?"

"I've been marching for two days without food and am very hungry." Henry replied, about to drop his rifle that was about his size and weight.

"Come right in." The man pleasantly replied.

Henry entered the tent. He dropped his rifle and stood there, watching the man walk to a camp chest. The man opened the chest and turned to Henry. "Help yourself, son." He said with a smile.

Henry eagerly reached into the chest and pulled out rations of hardtack, smoked meat, and apples. He ate heartily and momentarily forgot about his kind host.

After Henry finished eating the man took a hollowed-out gourd, filled it with water from a bucket in the corner of the tent, and handed it to Henry. "Would you like a drink of water?"

"Thank you sir." Henry said as he gratefully took the gourd. He took a big gulp of water and then looked the man in the eye. "You've been very kind to me, and I would like to know your name."

"My name is Lee." He responded.

"Lee-what Lee?" Henry stammered. "Not General Lee?"

"That is my name." The General quietly replied. He then held out his hand.

Henry took a step back out of admiration for the General. He wiped his dusty hands on his shirt and shook Lee's hand.

"What is your name, son?" General Lee asked.

"Henry Smith, sir."

"Well Henry, take care of yourself my boy." Lee said. He put his hand on Henry's shoulder and led him to the tent's opening.

"I will sir." Henry said. He looked in the General's kind eyes one final time. "Thank you again."

General Lee smiled, "Anytime."

With that, Henry began to march down the road with renewed energy. He was now ready to face anything for his General.

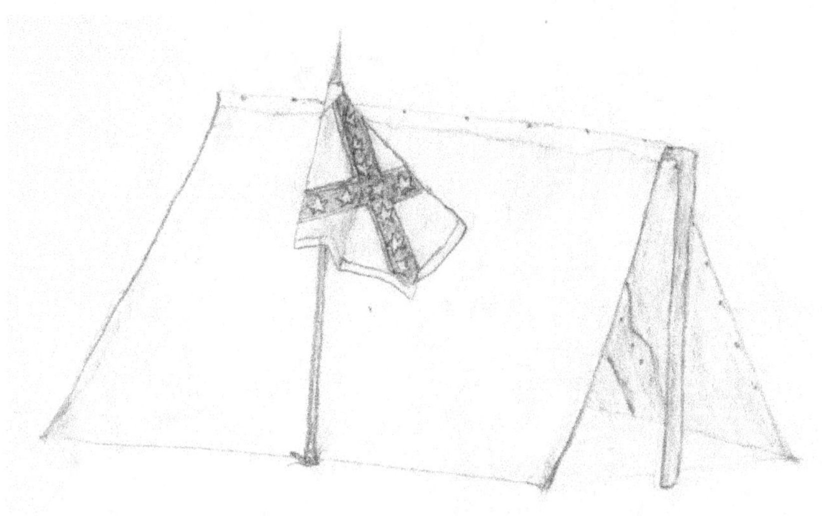

4. Lee at Gettysburg

July 2, 1863. Evening

Marcus Wright flopped down in pure exhaustion. He, along with his regiment, had been fighting at Gettysburg for the last two days in a row. He wiped the sweat out of his eyes with the back of his once-blue sleeve. His face was blackened with powder and dust, but he knew cleaning it would do nothing as long as the battle continued.

"What do you think?" A comrade asked as he sat down besides Marcus.

Marcus quickly glanced up. "John! Them Rebs haven't gotten you yet! I thought I saw you fall today." He said with a touch of relief.

"No. Not yet anyhow." John replied as he looked off over the distant battlefield. The sun had set, but in the twilight the soldiers could still see smoke rise from the field.

Marcus clenched his jaw. "I hate them Rebels. Hope every one of them dies. Leave their wounded out there, I don't care and never will. They deserve this. If I ever meet one alive he'll wish he never crossed paths with me. And if I could just glimpse General Lee I'll kill him." He said with anger. "Them Rebs killed one brother, and Joseph, my other brother, is probably dead too. They ruined my family!"

John slowly nodded as he continued to survey the battlefield. "I lost family to this war too. Lost a brother 'cause he joined the Confederacy."

Marcus shook his head in disbelief. "He's as good as dead then."

John nodded, then stood. He turned away. "We should get some rest. I doubt this battle is over."

Marcus stood. He clenched his jaw and looked out to the field. Smoke was still slowly rising, and the wounded and dead still covered the field. He shook his head and walked to a clump of bushes with some blankets spread beside them. He stiffly lowered himself on the ground and willed himself to fall asleep.

***

July 4, Morning.

Early the next morning Marcus jerked awake. The drums were tapping, calling everyone to arms. He sat up. There was no time to eat, as soldiers were all lining up, so Marcus grabbed his gun, pushed himself to his feet, and fell into rank.

A younger man leaned in to Marcus and asked, "Do yah know where we're fightin' today?"

Marcus shook his head, "No."

The Union soldiers gathered and waited for orders. On the other side of the field Marcus could see the gray uniforms of the Confederates line up and his bitterness flew up again.

His buddy John walked up and slapped Marcus on the back, "Let's give it to 'em."

Marcus gripped his gun tighter and nodded, gritting his teeth.

Their captain rode up at that moment. "Men, stand strong, we'll end this battle - and war - soon enough!"

At that the boys started cheering and they marched out to meet their foe. They lined up. Marcus loaded his gun and cocked it. He held it steady, with his finger on the trigger.

The order was given, "Fire!"

Marcus and his comrades all welcomed the Confederates with a volley of lead. And the third day of fighting at Gettysburg began.

The sun rose. Sunlight flashed off the men's guns, and sweat poured from the men's faces. The temperature steadily rose to over 90 degrees. Marcus wiped the sweat off his brow and paused to reload. As he did so his buddy John fell.

"John!" Marcus shouted. He bent over John, "....No!" Realizing nothing could be done, he resumed fighting. Waves of men on both sides fell. They were replaced by more men, only to be mowed down again. Yells, shouts, cannon blasts, and musket shots filled the field and echoed throughout the countryside.

"Press forward men!"

Marcus, among others, pressed forward, all the while firing his rifle.

Suddenly, something hit Marcus and spun him around. He felt himself sink to his knees, then everything went black.

***

Some time later, Marcus opened his eyes and found himself on his back. He heard shots being fired in the distance. He slowly shifted his position. His mind was fuzzy, but he realized he had been hit. He slowly moved his arms, then his legs, and stopped as searing pain shot up his left leg. He clenched his teeth and raised himself on his elbow to survey the damage. His leg was shattered, and he was lying in one of the many fields of Gettysburg. He was not sure what time it was, but judging from the sun it was late afternoon, and the fighting in his area had ended and moved on. Feeling faint from lack of water and loss of blood, he lowered himself back down. *Looks like we did a lot of damage...sure hope we whipped those Rebels good.*

As he lay there, he heard a horse approaching. He looked up, and to his side along the edge of the field came a solemn man riding a horse along with others who he assumed were officers.

"It's General Lee!" He murmured. A flicker of disgust ran through Marcus and he, with effort, raised his arms, looked Lee in the face, and said "Hurrah for the Union!"

Lee stopped and looked in Marcus' direction. He then dismounted and began slowly walking towards the young Union soldier lying on the ground.

He's going to kill me! Marcus initially thought as a wave of fear overtook him. But as the General approached, Marcus looked at his eyes. All he saw was extreme sadness and gentleness in them.

Lee walked right up to Marcus, took his hand, and said, "My son, I hope you will soon be well."

Marcus' eyes filled with tears. All words remained stuck in his throat. Lee straightened, walked back, mounted his horse, and continued towards his destination.

The hatred, bitterness, and anger he felt towards his foe earlier that day disappeared. He turned over and through his tears fell asleep.

Several hours later Marcus woke up and found himself in a crude field hospital within Gettysberg. He gathered his bearings and realized he was lying on a pile of straw on the ground. The tent was filled with the wounded, and he saw some nurses walking among them. He saw a doctor moving about, and noticed his leg was heavily bandaged.

A young soldier entered the tent and briefly spoke with the doctor there, then he hurriedly glanced around before noticing Marcus. He quickly walked over to him. "Marcus! Am I glad to see you!" He exclaimed as he carefully sat down beside Marcus.

Marcus squinted and looked up at him. "What? Joseph! You're alive!"

"More than you." Joseph said as the two brothers embraced. He looked around. "They treating you alright here?"

"Don't know a thing from when I fell asleep on the battlefield to waking up here. Might've fainted too for all I know." Marcus said. "Who won?"

"We did, though the Rebs put up a great fight." His brother replied as he ran his fingers through his hair. "It was a costly day. Don't want to be in another battle for the rest of my life."

Marcus nodded sympathetically. "At least you came out of this battle without a scrape."

Joseph placed his head in his hands. "Then I came upon a young Reb, must've been 16, wounded, and…" Joseph hesitated. He glanced up at Marcus nervously. "You'll probably hate me, but I had to give him water…poor kid probably died shortly after. I couldn't do anything more, was in the thick of the battle. Thought if it were me in his place, I'd appreciate help no matter who it was from!"

"I understand, Joseph. Them Rebs are people like you and me." Marcus calmly answered.

Joseph looked at Marcus closely. "Say, wha' happened to you? Last I saw you, you hated anything and anyone associated with the Rebs."

Marcus smiled, "Tell you what, come back tomorrow and I'll tell you."

"Alright. You better get some rest, and take care." Joseph said as he pushed himself up off the floor.

"Same to you." Marcus replied as they hugged once more.

Marcus watched his brother walk out, hoping it wasn't the last time he'd see him alive. He then shifted himself best he could and shut his eyes, reliving the moments of the day with General Lee.

5. Desolation to Brightness

Lieutenant William Obenchain rode into camp. He reigned in his horse, looked around, and dismounted. "Looks like it's just the two of us." He murmured to his horse. He shook the water from his eyes and looked up, hoping the rain would let up. Taking his horse's reins, he walked over to a hitching post by an empty tent, tied the reins to it, and beat his hands together. "I'm about frozen. How about we light a fire?"

He gathered several twigs and found some smoldering chunks of coal in a fire pit. After piling the twigs and coals together, William got on his knees on the soggy ground and began to blow on the coals to try and ignite the twigs.

A horse rode into camp, and William heard someone dismount. He remained on his knees, however, vigorously blowing on the coals. The ground rustled nearby, but William barely noticed. He eventually felt a person stop beside him to his right. *I'll look up when this fire is lit. It's so close I cannot stop blowing!* He thought while blowing harder.

"My boy, let me show you how to make that fire." A sympathetic voice said.

William instantly stopped blowing, and though he was lighthearted from blowing so hard he quickly stood, saluted, and stammered, "General Lee, I'm so sorry- I didn't realize it was you standing by me!"

General Lee smiled, "No need to worry." He crouched down by the forlorn soldier and fire pit. He took the wood off the top and said "Take the kindling and coals off the ground below the wood and lay them in the open." While William did so Lee continued, "This is the way I was taught to make a fire when I was a boy."

Within a few minutes a roaring fire was in the pit.The rain had stopped and William and Lee sat side by side, drying themselves by the fire.

"Thank you, General. Guess I'm no match for fire-starting." William said.

"Anytime. It can take some tries in wet weather." The General replied, his eyes crinkled up in a smile.

Other officers began to enter the camp and soon it transformed into a bustling area.

General Lee clasped William's shoulder, "I'll be seeing you around, Lieutenant."

William stood and saluted. "Yes sir."

Lee smiled, winked, and walked over to an officer while William remained behind.

"It is amazing how General Lee can turn a desolate, dreary, and lonely area into the most inviting place just by his presence."

William thought with a satisfied smile as he sat down again by the fire- Lee's fire.

Part 2: Acts of Mercy

6. Do Unto Others

Daniel, Peter, and other members of the Third Ohio Regiment huddled together on the cold ground, waiting for daylight to come. They were too tired, discouraged, and weak to care about anything. They were prisoners of the Confederates, heading for Richmond. On this particular evening, their captors stopped with them in a small Tennessee town. Peter looked at his comrades. He shook his head. How will they survive?

"Thinking?" Daniel asked, breaking Peter's thoughts.

"Yes. Here we are with the enemy. Nobody will pity us, nobody cares." Peter lamented, wrapping his tattered coat tighter around his shoulders. "It's so cold and wet, we can't even light a fire. Daniel, I'd rather die than go to a Rebel prison!" He cried.

"Now don't say such things." His friend said with a frown. But Daniel's shoulders sagged as well.

As they sat there, a group from the Fifty-Fourth Virginia Regiment came up. Curiosity overcame them, and they wanted to see some Yankee prisoners.

The leader of the Virginians surveyed the sad looking group. "Hi fellas."

The boys from Ohio glanced over cautiously. Daniel slowly lifted a hand in reply.

One of the Virginians leaned over to a comrade of his and whispered, "They're a sorry looking bunch. Maybe we should help?"

The Virginians huddled together, whispering what to do, while occasionally peeking at the forlorn captives. "Let's go back to camp and bring 'em some refreshment." The leader suggested. They all nodded eagerly in agreement and scurried off.

Daniel shrugged. "Guess they wanted to see some Yanks in a tight spot."

Nobody bothered to reply. They all continued sitting there, depressed and rejected. An occasional cough rose up from the group as the sun began setting and the air turned colder.

Shortly after, the captured soldiers heard tremendous whooping and hollering. They looked at each other, then looked in the direction of the sound. Suddenly a much larger group from the Fifty-Fourth Virginia regiment burst into view. They brought wagons filled with coffee, kettles, cornbread, and bacon, and stopped right in front of the captives.

The leader stepped forward. "We brought y'all some refreshments. Oh, and the name's Alden." He said while waving his arms in the direction of the wagons.

The captives apprehensively stood up.

"Daniel, is this a trap?" Peter muttered.

One of the Virginians closest to Peter heard the question. "Why, of course not! We're here to help! Come on!"

The captives' faces instantly brightened and they joined the Virginians to help unload the wagons.

"You didn't bring everything you have to eat, did you?" Daniel asked one of the soldiers.

"Eh, food will come, but the opportunity to help doesn't always come" The soldier nonchalantly replied while slapping Daniel on the back.

The captives slowly warmed up to their unlikely helpers and visitors, and they spent the rest of the night together. The next morning the captives were refreshed and stronger for the journey to Richmond.

Before leaving, Peter went to Alden and shook his hand. "We will forever be indebted to you all for your kindness towards us." He said, his voice catching.

Alden smiled brightly, "Anytime."

"We will never forget your kindness to us!" Different members of the Union prisoners cried out as they began to leave the town with their captors. The 54th Regiment of Virginians remained behind, waving hats, guns, and anything else they had as they bid farewell to their new and unlikely friends.

***

Several months later Peter, Daniel, and other Union captives were exchanged. They returned to their Ohio regiment and found themselves encamped near Kelley's Ferry on the Tennessee River. Shortly after the Battle of Missionary Ridge occurred, all Confederate captives were marched to Kelley's Ferry and ferried across the river. While the ferrying of prisoners was occurring, Peter, Daniel, and some others from the Third Ohio stood on the landing, observing the activity.

Peter nudged Daniel with his arm. "Figure any of our Virginian friends climbing out that boat are among the captives? They look like Virginians."

Daniel shrugged. "There's lots of regiments out there."

Before Daniel could comment further, Peter cupped his hands to his mouth. "Hello boys! What's your regiment?" He called out to the captives.

"The Fifty-fourth Virginia," was the reply.

The words had barely left the captives' mouths when Daniel, Peter, and the rest suddenly turned on their heels and rushed back to their camp, yelling, "The Fifty-fourth Virginia is at the ferry!"

This announcement caused great excitement. All men in the camp began running about wildly, picking up as much food they could lay their hands on. They collected coffee, bacon, sugar, beef, and preserved fruits, then headed off towards the ferry with a yell. They ran right into the middle of the prisoners from Virginia and hugged all of them like long-lost friends.

"You didn't forget us when we were captives, now we won't forget you!" Daniel declared. As he spun around, he came face to face with Alden. "Why, Alden! You came through that battle alright!" Daniel exclaimed as he grabbed his former Good Samaritan in an embrace.

"Yes sir I did, thankfully most of the boys in our regiment came through." Alden replied with a smile. He looked at Daniel. "I can't believe y'all didn't forget us."

Daniel waved his arms towards the plentiful supplies they brought. "We never forgot you. Now come! Eat! Rest!" He said as he led Alden towards the center of the activity.

These boys from Ohio then laid out a feast as never seen before for their rebel friends, and they had the happiest reunion ever.

7. Angel of Marye's Heights

December 11, 1862, Late Evening

Nineteen year old Confederate soldier Richard Kirkland lay on the frozen ground and tried to get some much-needed sleep. After fighting the Union soldiers for several days at Fredericksburg, he was exhausted and cold since it was the middle of December. However, sleep would not come. Richard rolled over and saw that his fellow comrade, John, was also wide awake.

"Do you hear them?" Richard asked.

"Oh sure," John replied, "It's just those Yankees moanin' at our wall. They all deserve it."

"What? No! Those poor wounded men...their doctors are not coming so far out to help them for fear of getting shot by us...and it's so cold out! Many of those men will probably die of the cold by tomorrow. Can't you see that these men are wounded? They're crying out for water!" Richard exclaimed in shock at the brutality of his comrade.

"Ah, but this is war. Regardless, you know that there ain't no way you'll be able to help. 'Sides, they all are Yankees! Nothin' but Yankees!"

"That out there could have easily been you!" Richard responded. "Also, my Lord died for these men, as well as for you and me! We all are rotten sinners but God sent His only Son, Jesus, to earth to live a perfect life and die on a cross in place of you and me! We deserve to die, but because Jesus took our place He can set us free if we turn to Him. He doesn't want anyone to perish without knowing Him! Those lives lying on the field are precious to Him, and to me...but what can I do to help?"

"Well at least it ain't me." John responded. "And as far as your Lord is concerned, I grew up constantly hearing tales about Him 'cause my parents believed in that stuff." He yawned and rolled over, "I'm goin' to bed."

Richard sighed and rolled over. *That easily could've been me! Oh Lord please show me what to do, help me be able to help those wounded men. Also, please have mercy on John! Save him!*

As he lay on the ground and tried to fall asleep, his mind wandered back to when he first enlisted. War seemed to be all glory to young Richard. A South Carolinian, he would eagerly keep track of the war and knew about every battle fought. Upon reaching the age of seventeen, many of his friends began to enlist into the Confederate army. Everyone would march off so grandly, in their gray coats with shiny brass buttons, getting a hero's welcome at every southern train station. It all seemed so grand that Richard never imagined the horrors these soldiers faced on the battlefield.

Eventually receiving the consent of his father, Richard immediately enlisted into the Confederate army - he was now ready to experience war. And what he experienced was very different from what he expected. Snapping back to where he was, Richard eventually fell asleep.

***

Several hours later in the early morning, as the soldiers wearily returned to their posts, hoping today they'd see the enemy gone, their brigade commander came to give them the battle plan.

"Okay y'all!" Richard's brigade commander, Joseph Kershaw, shouted. "These Yankees desire to fight some more, so let's go show them what we're made of!" With that, Kershaw walked around his men, repeating his words as well as trying to encourage them as they prepared for another day of battle.

Richard's eyes grew wide at the news; he was hoping that someone would surrender. He looked out to where the Yankees were preparing to attack and saw that the field between the two armies was still covered with wounded Northerners. *Those wounded, they...are still out there. I cannot bear to hear them crying out for help and water...it breaks my heart.*

He then took his place behind the stone wall, wiped the cold sweat off his brow, picked up his gun, and focused his eyes on the advancing Union army.

Fierce fighting began. The Union soldiers had to cross a field to reach the Confederates, who were fighting from behind a stone wall. Row after row of men fell before the Confederate wall. Cries of

"Water, please!" filled the air from the wounded. Richard gritted his teeth and continued fighting.

He then heard a wounded Northerner cry, "Water, please! If my friends cannot give me water, will my enemies give me some?" Richard couldn't bear it any longer. The words of Paul in the Bible came rushing through his head- "*If your enemy is hungry, feed him. If he is thirsty, give him something to drink.*" He stepped back in shock- this was a plea for mercy, and he knew he had to do something. He quickly slung his gun over his shoulder and ran to where his commander, General Kershaw, was staying.

Meanwhile, over at General Kershaw's headquarters, Gen. Joseph Kershaw was standing at the second story window of a nearby house, monitoring the battle. He paced back and forth, when suddenly some movement in his ranks caused him to press his forehead into the window's glass. "Who is that? Someone fleeing battle? No, wait, he is coming here!" With that, Kershaw thundered down the stairs and nearly ran into a breathless Richard Kirkland.

"Sir, I'm Private Kirkland." He saluted then rushed into his request. "I can't bear hearing those poor people begging for water. May I please go over the wall and give those wounded men water?"

General Kershaw looked at Richard in shock. "Kirkland, don't you know that you would get a bullet through your head the minute you stepped over the wall?"

"Yes sir, I know that; but if you will let me, I am willing to try it." Richard replied.

Kershaw, moved by this young man's compassion, reluctantly replied, "Kirkland, the enemy is behind you with guns ready to take your life, but if you will, go and may God protect you."

"Thank you! Oh thank you sir!" Richard's face broke out into a huge smile as he saluted and ran out. *Thank You Father!* He prayed as he sprinted back to the Confederate battle lines.

Richard quickly began to gather as many canteens as he could. "Let me see...there is another canteen! Excuse me sir," Richard said as he addressed a soldier nearby, "May I borrow your canteen?"

"Well, why would you need it?"

"Please sir," pleaded Richard, "I'm going to relieve those men." He gestured to the wounded laying before the Confederate wall.

"Go ahead, take it." The man replied, looking Kirkland up and down, "Say, you really think that the enemy won't see you? There is an open field between them and us, you know. They can see a flea jumping in the middle, but you think they will miss seeing you?"

"I understand the risk, however, I know that my Lord will be with me. And He is in charge of my life." Richard then ran off to gather more canteens.

"Ok, whatever you believe." The man replied as curiosity overtook him. He kept his eyes on the young soldier and peeked over the wall to see what would happen to Richard.

Upon gathering about a dozen canteens, Richard walked up to the wall. Bullets whizzed around him, cannons boomed, shells cracked, men fell. He took a deep breath, placed a hand on the wall, and jumped over.

"Hey!" A Union officer yelled, "There goes a rebel to rob our wounded and dead! Fire upon him!" Bullets splattered the dust by Richard.

Father, if it is your will, please spare me, so I may help these men. Kirkland prayed as he quickly made his way to the nearest wounded man. He knelt by him, lifted his head, and placed it on his lap. "Here, sir, drink some water."

The man looked up with feverish eyes at Richard's face, "Why...are you...helping me...a Northerner?" He asked through parched lips and gritted teeth.

"Here now, don't speak. I'm here to help. You're wounded, and it doesn't matter whether you are a Northerner or Confederate. You're a person created by the Lord. A life that matters." As he spoke, Richard took the man's knapsack and placed it under his head. He then took the man's injured leg and gently wrapped it with some cloth.

He stood up and made his way to another wounded Northerner who was barely waving an arm, signaling that he was still alive and needed water. Richard went over to the man while dodging flying bullets. He knelt by the man, tenderly lifted his head, and poured the reviving liquid down the man's throat. The wounded Northerner looked up, his eyes filled with tears. Richard gently told him to not speak, as he lowered his head down onto his knapsack. Richard then straightened the man's broken arm and moved on.

By this time, the Union commander realized what Richard was doing and he shouted, "Stop firing! That man is too brave to die!" Men from both sides slowly stopped fighting, and for the next two hours the field was silent, with everyone's eyes on Richard, their mouths hanging half open in shock.

Holding his last canteen of water, Richard hurried toward another wounded man. He knelt beside him onto the icy, snow-covered ground. "Here, take some water. I'm here to help you as much as I can."

The man looked up at Richard and tears filled his eyes. "Sir," he whispered, "you're like an angel sent to me in this hour. No one up to this point has even cared to help me. I've been laying here all night and day."

"Sir, that's what compelled me to come here to you." Richard responded as he covered the man with a coat and bound his wounded head.

He stood up and ran to refill his canteens. By this point cries of "Water, here!" filled the field. Those too weak to speak lifted a hand, but Richard noticed everyone.

Nearly two hours later Kirkland finished administering aid and giving water to the wounded soldiers, so he went back to his position, his heart bursting with joy, *Thank you! Oh, thank you Father!* he inwardly exclaimed. Tears ran down his face, mingled with dirt and sweat. Both sides erupted in cheers, commending this "Angel of Marye's Heights" who was willing to risk his life to save the enemy.

Although Richard's act saved lives, the battle wasn't over, and he had to continue fighting. But he would stop and help any one of his fellow soldiers who fell. All of a sudden, he heard a soldier cry out. Richard quickly looked around, and immediately located a fallen Confederate about 30 feet from him. He quickly made his way over, and knelt down by the soldier. This soldier's face was covered in sweat, dust, and gunpowder. His hands were deathly cold, and he was heavily bleeding from a gunshot wound in the thigh. Richard hardly recognized this man as being from his own regiment. "Here, let me help."

At the sound of Richard's voice, the soldier's eyes fluttered open, and Richard gasped. He recognized those eyes. "John?" he exclaimed. The conversation he had the evening before came tumbling back into his head.

"Richard...I am such a fool for what I told...you last night...That was so wrong...of me. Please..."

Richard looked John in the eye, "I have already forgiven you, my friend."

John looked up at Richard, "Richard, everything my mother told me...came back into my head...when I saw you jump over the wall." He stopped, drew in a sharp breath, and continued. "The message of Jesus coming to earth to die for me all made sense...you were willing to help the enemy no matter the cost, just like Jesus did for me."

Richard's eyes filled with tears, "Praise the Lord! I've prayed for this day to come! Here, let me give you some water." Richard lifted John's head and poured water down his throat. He then wrapped

John's leg with a cloth. "Let me find someone to help bring you to the hospital."

"Thank you Richard. What have I to fear now?"

"Nothing, for God is in control, my new brother in Christ." Richard replied as he got up to find some soldiers to help. A big smile nearly split Richard's face in two as he exclaimed "Praise the Lord!"

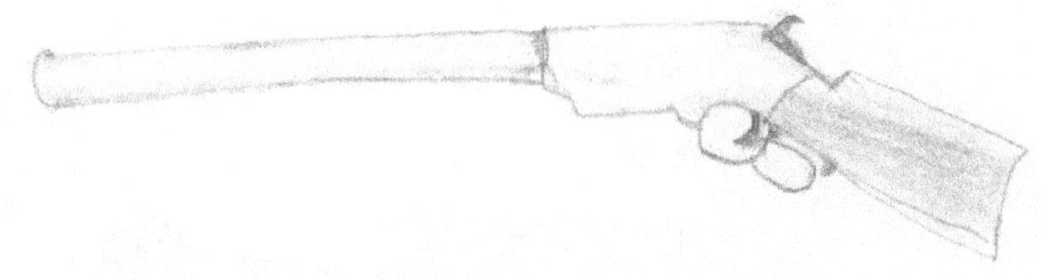

8. Brothers at Heart

Lieutenant Sterling ran his arm across his eyes to clear the sweat out of them. It was the first day of the Battle of Shiloh, and it was also his regiment's first battle. It was around three in the afternoon, and bullets were raining down upon his regiment, who was charging for a bluff.

Sterling shot his gun while running through the woods for the protective bluff overlooking the Tennessee River. Someone beside him tripped on the thick underbrush and fell against Sterling. Sterling staggered then steadied the man who fell.

"I'm so sorry sir!" The younger soldier gasped.

"No harm done." Starling replied as the group of soldiers surged for the protective bluff. As he stumbled into the protective area, he leaned over to catch his breath. The young soldier who tripped in the woods stopped by Sterling to rest as well.

Sterling looked up. "I wasn't sure we were gonna make it." He looked at the young soldier again, "Hey! You're Dan Smith! I didn't know they sent you here!"

The soldier looked at Sterling with surprise. "Sterling, my ol' pal! Last I saw you was over at the church service in Texas before joinin' the army. Great to see a familiar face out here." The man replied with a southern drawl.

As the two men rested and caught up with each other, an officer walked over with a bunch of canteens slung around his arms. "Men, I need you both to go to the rear with our company's canteens to refill them with water."

"Yes sir." Sterling and Dan said in unison while standing up. They took the canteens and began walking down the hill behind the bluff to the rear. After several minutes of walking both soldiers' foreheads became drenched in perspiration.

"It is so hot, I bet you could cut through this air with a knife." Dan muttered while wiping his forehead with his shirt.

Sterling breathed in the muggy air and looked up between the trees, "Looks like it'll rain."

"Sure hope so." Dan replied as the two continued walking in silence, stepping around debris.

As the two men approached the rear, Sterling abruptly stopped. "Dan, listen."

Dan stopped and strained his ears. "What?"

"Someone's quietly groaning."

Sterling followed the sound, which led to a wounded Union soldier lying on the ground. Dan followed behind. The man was wearing a captain's uniform, and one of his legs was oddly twisted beneath him.

Both soldiers knelt by the man, whose face filled with fear. "Sir, can we do anything for you?" Sterling asked.

The Union captain took a deep breath. "Oh, sirs, I'd be most grateful if you would straighten out my leg, since it's badly shot and the pain is killing me."

"Of course," Sterling replied and immediately took action. "Dan, grab under his arms and hold tight. I'm gonna grab the leg and straighten it." Dan quickly got into position. Sterling took the man's ankle and gave it a quick twist and pull. The wounded man passed out, and Sterling looked up. "Better knocked out than awake right now." He muttered to Dan. "Let's set up a bed of sorts under that large tree. We can drag this man over for some shade."

The two comrades stood and began gathering and piling leaves under the tree. As Sterling was gathering some more leaves a wounded soldier feebly called out to him, "Sir, you got extra water on you?"

Sterling stopped and crouched down by him, "I'm so sorry but I don't have any water. If you wait a moment I'll fetch you some. Here, let me take your canteen."

"Thank you." The young soldier replied as he handed Sterling his canteen.

Beside him lay another soldier. Sterling turned to him, "Do you need anything?"

"Nothin much..it's just that the sun is burning me right up, and I can't move." He replied.

Sterling nodded. "I'll come back and see what I can do for y'all. Give me a moment." He stood and went over to Dan.

"Got the bed ready?"

"Yup." Dan replied, wiping his dusty hands on his pants.

"Great, let's go move that man."

The two soldiers walked back to where they left the Union captain. He had come to, but seemed to be fading fast.

"Sir, we've prepared a bed under a tree with shade for you. Mind if we move you over?' Dan asked.

"Go ahead." The man quietly replied.

After bringing the captain over to the tree, Sterling asked, "Is there anything else we can do for your comfort?"

"I'd be most obliged if you brought those two wounded men lying over there by me- they're from my company and we can all assist each other if we are together."

"Certainly, sir." Sterling replied. "I was just talking to them both."

Dan gathered more leaves to enlarge the bed. They then brought the two wounded men over and laid them on either side of the captain.

As Sterling straightened, he noticed the captain was wearing a heavy gold watch with a chain that extended around his neck.

"Here, sir, let me put this watch in your pocket so nobody robs you of it." Sterling said.

"Oh no, you take it off and keep it. I'm sure I cannot recover, and I want you to keep it for your kindness to us." The man replied.

"No, I cannot do that." Sterling replied while gently removing the watch and placing it in the captain's pocket. He then reached over and took the three men's canteens. "Dan and I will return with water." Sterling said. He stood up and the two soldiers continued their walk towards the rear. "Hey, Dan, let's gather some haversacks dropped in the battle for those soldiers."

"Alright." His friend replied. They quickly found three haversacks that they picked up and slung over their shoulders.

Eventually, a small stream came into view. "Water!" Dan cried. He dropped the canteens and ran into the stream, splashing himself with water.

Sterling grinned and shook his head good-naturedly. "Dan! We need to fill these canteens! We're on a mission."

"Yes, sir," Dan said while returning to Sterling. "Least I'm all refreshed! You should give it a try." He grabbed a canteen to fill it with water.

Soon, the two comrades filled all the canteens and began walking back to where they left the three Union soldiers.

Upon returning to the soldiers Sterling and Dan crouched by them. "Here are your canteens. And here's some food we gathered too." Sterling said.

"Oh, thank you sirs!" The young soldiers said while eagerly taking the canteens and haversacks.

The wounded captain quietly spoke up, "Since you were so kind to us, would you both mind signing your names in our memorandum books?"

"We'd be happy to sign." Sterling said. Dan nodded in approval. They took the soldiers' books, signed their names and included their regiment, the 2nd Texas Infantry, beside their names. Upon handing the books back, the three wounded men looked at the signatures and then looked up with shock at Sterling and Dan.

"Are you really Texans?" The captain asked.

"Yes we are." Dan replied..

"All of us had prayed we would never fall into the hands of Texans because we heard you all butcher your enemies."

"Well, did we not fight you like men? And are not the brave always kind?" Sterling tactfully replied.

One of the wounded beside the captain quietly spoke up, "Surely your kindness cannot be questioned, and we cannot express our gratitude for it."

"Where are y'all from?" Dan asked.

"Illinois." Replied the captain.

As they spoke, Sterling noticed one of their corps's ambulances nearby. He waved his arms to attract their attention. The driver of the ambulance noticed him and came over.

"Sir, we have some wounded Yanks here, if y'all would take them and take good care of them." Sterling said. He turned to the Union soldiers. "It was a pleasure meeting you. Our folks'll take good care of y'all."

"Thank you again, sirs!" They called as Sterling and Dan began to tramp back to their regiment with water.

***

After this event, Sterling and Dan's regiment fought through many more battles and eventually ended up at the siege of Vicksburg. It was the end of May, around midnight, and Sterling and Dan were fast asleep in a trench. They suddenly jerked awake amid the call to arms, and the entire ridge before them lit up with musket fire. Minnie balls and shells screamed through the air, with both sides aimlessly firing at each other. Sterling, though exhausted, picked up his gun and began mechanically loading and shooting.

As he paused to reload, the trench he was in lit up and Sterling was knocked off his feet. Pain shot up his left ankle, hips, and entire back. Dan was farther away so the shell explosion missed him. He ran over to Sterling. "Sterlin'! You alright?" He asked as he shook Sterling's arm.

Sterling looked up at his friend, "Suppose it's 'bout time I got hit." He quietly said before slipping into unconsciousness.

Dan looked around desperately and quickly turned to another comrade behind him. "Help me carry Sterling over to the surgeon."

Dan took his jacket off, and rolled Sterling onto it. He then took one end, and the soldier took the other, and they half-dragged, half-carried him to the rear through the rain of lead.

Dan and the other man placed Sterling on the ground outside the makeshift hospital, and Dan went inside to talk to the surgeon. He then came out and knelt by Sterling. "The surgeon will come out. I'll be back to check in on you."

Sterling looked at Dan and took his hand "Thank you." He whispered through clenched teeth. He remained on Dan's coat and helplessly watched his friend leave into the woods back to the thick of the fighting.

***

The siege of Vicksburg lasted another 47 days. During this time Sterling remained on the edge of life and death, battling the summer heat, flying bullets, starvation, and pain as the Confederate surgeons ran out of medical items due to the siege.

Upon the surrender of the city Sterling's comrades all entered the hospital and found him lying on a cot. They filed by, laying coins by him and whispering "God bless" as they walked out, possibly forever, because the Union had taken the city.

Sterling and the other wounded Confederate soldiers were then moved to an old mansion on a hill where Union soldiers and surgeons were located. As Sterling lay on his cot, he glanced around with despair. *There is not a friend I know or a hand that will help me now.*

***

Several days later a young Union guard stuck his head into the ward where Sterling and others were kept. "Are there any Texans here?" He asked.

John, a man besides Sterling spoke up. "Yes siree there are."

The guard stepped in. "Are there any of the Second Texas Infantry here, do you know?"

"Right there." John said while pointing to Sterling.

The guard walked to Sterling's bedside. "Do you belong to the Second Texas Infantry?"

Sterling hesitantly looked up at him. "I do."

"Were you in the battle of Shiloh?"

"I was." Sterling replied.

"Did your regiment wear white cloth clothes in that battle?" The guard asked intently.

"Um....it did."

The guard's rifle slipped from his hand, its butt thumping the floor. He reached into his shirt's pocket and pulled out a worn, black memorandum book. He quickly flipped to a page, put it before Sterling, and nervously asked, "Do you know the men whose names are written there?"

Sterling took the book with a trembling hand. He steadied his arm and let his eyes focus on the page. "I do; the first name is mine, the other Dan Smith's, of my company."

The guard's lips trembled, he cleared his throat. "Do you know me?"

Sterling looked the man in the face. "I do not."

"Did you write that?"

"Well, that's my handwriting."

"Do you remember picking up three men an' putting 'em on a bed of leaves in the shade, and giv'n 'em water an' something to eat, an' tak'n a watch off the captain an' putting it in his pocket, an' then putting 'em in an ambulance an' send'n off to the hospital?" He quickly asked.

"Yes."

"I'm one of 'em." The guard said as tears began running down his face. He leaned over and embraced Sterling. A shocked Sterling found tears running down his face as well as he returned the embrace.

The guard straightened himself. "You saved my life and that of my captain and comrade," his voice cracked, "and I have hunted for you or some from your command on every battlefield since, so I might prove myself as true to you. Now, what can I do for you? I'm ready to do anything that I can."

"Nothing." Sterling slowly replied.

"But I must do something. Do you need money?" The guard pulled a wallet out. "You must, for you are in our lines now and your money is worthless."

"No, no, I have plenty of money, given to me by my comrades when they left me."

"Well, you need clothing?"

"No, I cannot sit up; and though my clothes were torn to shreds when I was wounded, I don't need more clothes until I am able to be up, which won't happen for many months."

The guard sat on the end of Sterling's bed. "Tell me how you were wounded."

Sterling proceeded to tell his new friend the details of his injury. The guard listened with the attentiveness and sympathy of a brother. When Sterling finished, the guard leaned in. "Are the surgeons kind to you?"

"Yes sir, they are. Everyone is kind to me." Sterling replied.

"Oh, they will be kinder and better still when I tell them who you are and what you did for me. I have never forgotten your kindness or your face." The guard excitedly said. "Oh, do you need better food?" He added as an afterthought.

Sterling faintly smiled and shook his head. "No, I've been well fed and cared for."

The guard nodded and stood up abruptly. "I must bring in some of our officers and tell them who you are, and from now on you'll be treated well. I know you will." He briskly walked out the room, and shortly reappeared with the Federal surgeon in charge of the hospital, along with several other officers. "Here is the man who saved my life!" He eagerly said while leading the group to Sterling's side. "You want to tell them the story, Sterling?"

"You go ahead and say it, since you experienced it." Sterling smiled while sinking back on his cot.

The guard leapt into the entire story with gusto. Everyone's attention in the room was drawn to him. He told of how he was wounded, how Sterling and his comrade, his enemies, helped him, and how they have met yet again. There was hardly a dry eye left in the room by the end of the account.

The surgeon bent over Sterling, "We'll treat you like one of our own soldiers. You have no need to fear."

Sterling was overcome with emotion. "I...I don't know what to say. Y'all have been too kind. Thank you." He said quietly.

The surgeon nodded, and he and the rest brought in by the guard walked out. Sterling looked at the guard. "Thank you."

"It's the least I can do." The guard replied with a shrug and a twinkle in his eyes. He walked out, leaving a still shocked Sterling behind with his thoughts.

Moments later, the guard returned, his arms overflowing with canned fruit, other delicacies, blankets, and sheets. Sterling haltingly lifted himself on his elbow. "What's this?"

"For you." The guard replied as he lowered the items on the bed with a flourish.

A smile nearly split Sterling's face. "You've been more than kind. Thank you."

The guard placed his hands on Sterling's bed. "This war may have placed us on opposite sides, but we are still brothers." He put his hand out. Sterling took it and they both shook hands.

"Indeed, y'all are our brothers." Sterling said with gratitude. "Brothers at heart."

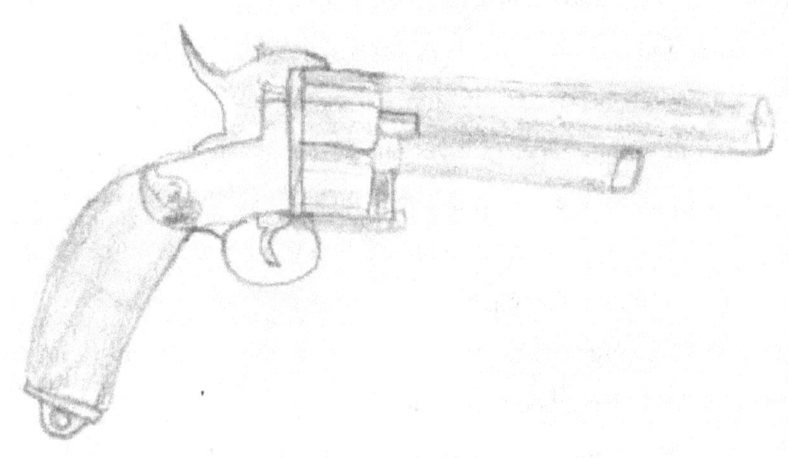

Part 3: President Lincoln and the Union

9. Lincoln and the Confederate

Nurse Lydia entered the hospital early one Saturday. Ever since the First and then Second Battles of Bull Run, the hospitals in Washington D.C. were overflowing with wounded, both Union and Confederate. She lost count of all the soldiers she helped, and everything merely went by in a blur. She walked over to the nurses' quarters.

"Good morning, Nancy." She called as cheerfully as she could to a tired looking nurse. "How'd the night shift go?"

"Hard. But worthwhile, if I can do anything to help these fellows out." The nurse replied as she stifled a yawn. "I'm going to catch several minutes of sleep before joinin' you all for the day." She sat on a small cot and leaned her head against the wall.

Lydia nodded sympathetically, "Get some rest."

"Oh, and we have a new case, though I think it's hopeless…a wounded Confederate." Nancy added before falling sound asleep.

As the day progressed and evening fell, a great commotion was heard by the door. Lydia ran to see what was wrong and gasped. "President Lincoln!" She whispered as she watched the tall man enter the hospital.

A surgeon came up to her at that moment, "President Lincoln is here to comfort the wounded. He visited every hospital so far in the city. Don't get in his way."

"Yes sir," Lydia said as she moved further back to be able to watch the President on his errand of comfort and mercy.

President Lincoln would stop, bend over, and sometimes kneel besides a cot. He shook hands, and made time to speak with every soldier.

She then saw him approach the cot where the new patient - the young Confederate - lay. Nancy was right, throughout the day he had been in much pain and seemed to be fading fast. Lydia held her breath to see what Lincoln would do. *He'll probably bypass him...he is our enemy.* She thought as she leaned against the wall.

However, Lincoln walked up beside the Confederate and knelt at his cot. He bowed his head, and, to Lydia's surprise, prayed for this dying soldier. He then stood, patted the boy's shoulder, and moved on. Before long he moved out of Lydia's ward and continued on his mission.

Lydia suddenly realized she forgot about the wounded the whole time Lincoln was in her ward, so she quickly went among them and checked on them. As she approached the Confederate lad, he feebly raised an arm up to her. "Ma'am," he whispered.

She took his arm and leaned forward, "Yes?"

"Please, can Mr. Lincoln come again?" He rasped. "Please?" He pleadingly looked in Lydia's eyes.

"I'll try and get him back." She promised as she turned and ran out the ward. She glanced out a window, and saw Lincoln was entering a carriage. She grabbed the hospital door and burst outside. "President Lincoln!" She called. The guards around him protectively moved closer to the president.

He looked at her. Though his face was weary and drawn, he smiled. "What is it?"

"Sir, that Rebel boy you prayed with is begging that you come again to him."

Lincoln's face lit up. He instantly got out of the carriage and hurried past Lydia back into the hospital. As she quickly followed behind, Lydia saw him grasp the arm of the boy, asking, "What can I do for you?"

The soldier looked up at Lincoln, "I am so lonely and friendless, Mr. Lincoln," he whispered, "and I am hoping that you can tell me what my mother would want me to say and do now."

Lincoln knelt by the bed. "Yes, my boy. I know exactly what your mother would want you to say and do. And I am glad that you sent for me to come back to you. Now, as I kneel here, please repeat the words after me." He said as he placed his arms on the youth's bed.

And so, while the young soldier rested his head upon Abraham Lincoln's arm, he repeated with his only present friend the words his mother taught him as a child:

Now I lay me down to sleep;

I pray the Lord my soul to keep.

If I should die before I wake,

I pray the Lord my soul to take.

And this I ask for Jesus' sake.

Lydia turned her head from the scene before her to hide her tears. What a kind-hearted man President Lincoln was.

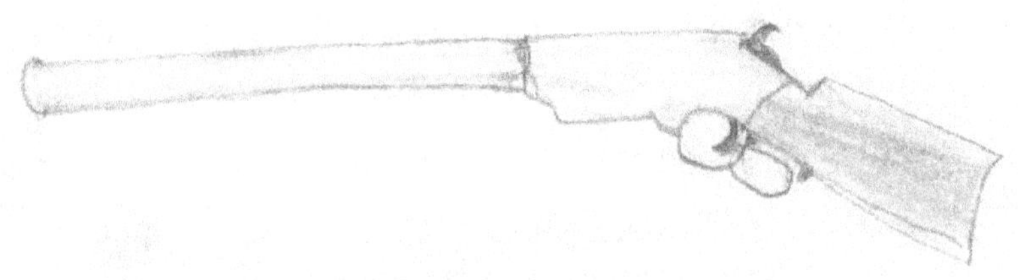

10. Mistaken Identity

Secretary of War, Mr. Stanton, stood outside the tent while straightening his clothes. He was about to meet General Grant and his staff in person for the first time, and he wanted to leave a good impression. He took a deep breath and entered the tent.

It took several seconds for his eyes to adjust to the darkness of the tent, but as his eyes cleared he saw several men standing at attention before him. One in particular was dressed rather commonly, and the other was elaborately dressed. Stanton, without a moment's hesitation, walked up to the finely dressed man and shook his hand, saying, "How are you, General Grant? I recognized you at first sight from your pictures!"

The man looked questioningly at the simpler dressed man beside him. "Actually, sir-" he began before the plain man interrupted. "Mr. Stanton, I appreciate your greetings, however I am Grant."

Stanton looked from one to the other, "I-I-I'm very sorry, sir." He stuttered while turning to shake Grant's hand.

Grant chuckled. "Though I'm certain Mr. Jennings, our surgeon, doesn't mind the error."

The finely dressed man smiled, "General Grant doesn't have a liking for fine military dress. He prefers to blend in with others."

Stanton nodded, "Well, now I know." He humbly replied.

11. Why Don't You Laugh?

Abraham Lincoln leaned back in his seat while reading a book. He occasionally looked up, expecting members of his cabinet to enter at any moment. He had called them in for a special meeting, but in the meantime, he kept himself occupied with the contents of the book. He could feel a smile occasionally crawl up his face as he read, but restrained himself from laughing out loud.

A loud knock brought him back to the matter at hand. President Lincoln waved an arm to a guard by the door, "Let them in." He calmly said as he directed his attention back to his book.

The door opened and Lincoln's cabinet members all solemnly walked in. They silently took their seats, and waited for the President to speak.

Lincoln, when he noticed that everyone was seated, looked at them and nodded. Then he turned the page of his book and began reading a short, humorous story out loud. Several lines into the story he burst out laughing. By the end of the story, Lincoln was laughing so hard he nearly dropped the book. But his cabinet members remained with the same stony, serious faces as when they entered.

Lincoln, noticing the story had no effect on his audience, turned the page and found another humorous story. He proceeded to read it out loud again, and by the end of the story he was in tears from laughing so hard. However, his cabinet members remained silent and serious.

After composing himself, Lincoln set the book down on a small table and leaned forward towards the men. "Gentlemen, why don't you laugh? With the fearful strain that is upon me night and day, if I did not laugh I should die, and you need this medicine as much as I do."

He then turned towards another document besides the book and picked it up. "I called this meeting to gain your thoughts on this document I recently drafted, a proclamation to free the slaves. However, laughter helps clear the mind before such monumental meetings. I suggest you all learn to occasionally laugh." He said with a smile.

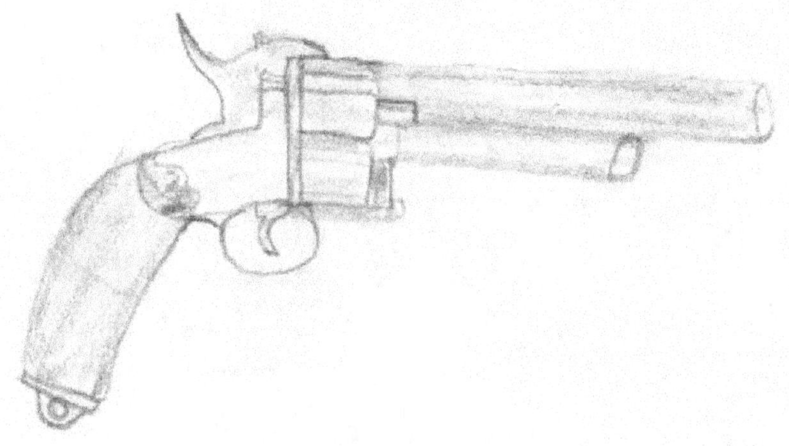

Part 4: Humorous Incidents

12. Gone Fishing

Mark abruptly woke up early one morning to the sound of a bugle ringing in his ear. "Argh!" He cried, surprised, as he rolled out of his cot as quickly as possible. His comrade, Thomas, was standing by the bed with a wide grin and a bugle in his hand. "Thomas!" Mark glared at him.

"Knew you'd need a firmer awakening. Somethin's afoot in camp this mornin' an' I thought you'd like to check it out." Thomas said while nonchalantly leaning backwards. "I'll meet you at the low wall surrounding that pond by the camp," he added mysteriously.

***

About ten minutes later Mark arrived at the pond and wall. He glanced around. "Tom!" He whispered. "Where are you?"

"Psst! Behind this tree!" His friend replied.

As Mark made his way over a slight movement caught his eye. He strained in the early morning light to see. There appeared to be a soldier sitting on the wall, and it looked like he was fishing. Mark shrugged and went over to his friend. "Thomas? You see that fellow?" he whispered.

"Yup. That's wha' we came to see."

"He's just fishin." Mark said, but his curiosity was aroused. The fishing soldier seemed to have forgotten his surroundings. He was using his gun as a rod, and would methodically lift the gun and examine the string attached to it. Mark looked closer. A bayonet was attached to the bottom of the string! "Tom, that fellow's nuts. Nobody can catch fish like that! And look how he examines that rod, string, and bayonet, as if he'll catch something!"

"Exactly." Thomas grinned. "Somethin's afoot. Let's go get breakfast. I doubt he'll leave, 'specially if he's lost his senses."

The sun came up and the camp was aroused. All the soldiers began preparing breakfast. As Mark joined some friends seated around a fire, one of the boys commented. "Say, did any of ya see that man fishin'?"

"Yes." Mark replied. "Let's go down after to see if he's still there!"

After breakfast the group of soldiers headed out to watch the spectacle. On the way others joined, so by the time they arrived quite a group had gathered.

The man was still there, regularly lifting his pole, examining it, and putting it back in the water.

Thomas joined Mark. "Wonder what's lacking in his mind?"

Mark shrugged. "Probably a lot!"

The group of soldiers began teasing and jesting, trying to get a reply from the man. Yet no response was given.

"Tom, I'm goin' to get the captain." Mark said.

"Alrighty! I can't wait to see his face!" Thomas whooped while the group burst out laughing.

Mark reached the captain's headquarters and noticed the captain was outside, drinking coffee.

"Soldier, everything alright down there? There's quite the racket going on!"

"Well sir, yes, I mean, no, I mean, how about you follow me?" Mark stuttered.

The captain put his cup down and followed Mark to the pond. Upon arriving he marched right through the crowd to the edge of the pond. He stopped, gaped, rubbed his eyes, and turned back to the crowd. "What's going on here?"

"Sir, that man!" A soldier replied before bursting out in laughter.

The captain turned back to the fishing soldier who still acted like he was the only person out there. "What are you doing here?" he demanded.

No response. The gun was lifted, examined, and dropped with the same regularity.

"Halt!" The captain said turning red.

No response. Up came the string and bayonet again.

Maybe hearing an accustomed order will knock him back to his senses, the captain thought. "Shoulder arms!"

The soldier continued sitting there with the same expression glued on the string, methodically lifting and dropping it into the water.

The captain turned around in frustration. "I'm going to get the colonel!" He threatened as he marched off. He had not gone far when he ran right into the colonel.

"Sir!" The captain spluttered.

"No need, I'm going to see what's the matter with that fellow." The colonel replied as he walked to the water's edge.

"Halt!" The colonel commanded the fisherman.

No response. The man's gaze remained fixed on his string.

"March!"

Yet again, no response. The gun continued to be lifted regularly, the bayonet examined, and then dropped back into the water by the man. The crowd burst out into fits of laughter.

The colonel looked around. "You!" He pointed to Mark. "Go get the surgeon!"

"Yes sir!" Mark immediately turned and ran back to the surgeon's tent.

The surgeon was outside, sorting different instruments in a bag. He looked up as Mark approached. "Need anything, son?" He asked kindly.

"Yes sir, the colonel has commanded that you follow me down to the water. Bring your bag."

The surgeon looked at Mark inquisitively but stood, bringing his medical bag along. As they approached the pond the surgeon bit his lip to keep from laughing at the comical scene before him. The crowd of boys was nearly in tears from laughing, the colonel and captain's faces were nearly purple, and the man sitting on the wall was as serious as ever, watching his fishing pole.

"Sir, you asked for me?" The surgeon asked while briskly approaching the colonel.

"Yes, check this man." The colonel replied, exasperated.

The surgeon set to work, examining the man as best as he could. "Sir, would you kindly stop your fishing so I can examine you?" He quietly asked.

No response. The man continued lifting the pole and dropping it with the same regularity as when he began.

After attempting to examine the patient, the surgeon turned around to face the captain. "Sir, I recommend that you give this insane fisherman a discharge. He is unfit for duty."

The captain nodded. "Alright." He proceeded to have an aide write out a discharge. The captain then took the paper, but before giving it to the man he paused. "What are you fishing for?" he asked.

No reply.

"Well, I guess you can give him the document," said the colonel.

The captain waved the paper in front of the fisherman. "Here! Take this!" He said loudly.

The fisherman grabbed the paper. "That's what I was fishing for!" He cried as he threw down his gun, placed the document in his pocket, and ran out of camp.

The group of soldiers burst out in more laughter. They began leaning on each other for support.

"Have...you...ever...seen...anything...like...that...before?" Thomas gasped to Mark.

"Never," Mark replied, greatly amused.

The captain, colonel, and surgeon stood there in shock, their mouths wide open.

"Well sir," the colonel finally said to the captain. "I've never seen such a thing in my life."

The captain nodded, unable to reply.

The surgeon burst out laughing. "That was the best thing I've seen in my whole life!" He chuckled as he walked over to the group of laughing soldiers.

The captain slowly grinned. "I suppose it was."

13. A Heart Stopping Escapade

Seventeen year old Kellie rode into the small town of Hamilton, Georgia. Dusk was falling, so he slowed down his horse and pondered whether to continue or stop for the night. As he glanced at the small shops lining the road, he saw activity at the entrance of one of them. The door opened and a man in Confederate uniform walked out. He casually walked with a slight limp to a horse and slowly mounted. Kellie rode up beside him. "Hello sir, which regiment are you with?" He asked.

The man looked at him. His eyes lit up. "Why, Kellie, I didn't ever expect to see you here!"

Kellie's jaw dropped, "Lieutenant Black, sir, I should've recognized you!"

The lieutenant chuckled. "It's been awhile. But I figured you were over in Atlanta with our regiment."

"I left on furlough with Smith to help him get back home after he was wounded. I'm heading back to our regiment now." Kellie said.

The lieutenant nodded and pointed to his leg. "I'm 'bout as patched up as I'll ever be. I'm going back too."

"Sir, could we go together? I've had several guards try to arrest me on conditions of desertion- if we were together, it would be better."

"Sounds good to me." The older soldier replied as the two picked up their horses' pace.

As they rode along, Kellie glanced at the countryside. War hadn't affected the area yet, and beautiful fields full of crops lined the road. As it got darker, he could hear coyotes in the distance. Owls hooted, and the air became cooler.

The lieutenant suddenly pulled back on his horse, surprising Kellie, who quickly stopped his horse, kicking up dust in the process. The lieutenant waited until Kellie came beside him, then he pointed to a house far back from the road. "Let's see if they'll take us in for the night." He said as he slowly spurred his horse forward.

Kellie silently followed. He was exhausted, and was glad his lieutenant was taking the lead. As they approached the home, Kellie looked around in admiration. The home had two stories and was surrounded by an ornate gate. The two soldiers stopped at the gate and waited. Presently, an older gentleman opened the house's door and looked out. "Hello! How may I help you?" He called.

"Good evening sir. We're just two soldiers heading back to our command and need a place to lay our heads for the night." The lieutenant called out.

The man fully opened the door and stepped out. He ran to the gate and opened the doors. "By all means please come in!" He eagerly said. "Have several young uns' myself in the army."

Kelley grinned at the lieutenant as both men dismounted. Their host took their horses' reins, tied them to a nearby post, and motioned that the soldiers follow him into the house. "Dinner is just being served." He said as he led the way into the home. As the soldiers followed close behind, they entered a dining room, where their host eagerly shouted, "Martha! Curtis! Mary! Everyone! We have company!"

There were about six or seven people seated at the table, Kelley noticed, and they quietly smiled and made room for the soldiers to sit.

"Welcome, sirs," One of the women stood- their host's wife, Kelley assumed.

As the two soldiers nodded at all the people and nervously sat down, their host waved his hand, "Eat as much as you'd like. I'll go tend to your horses." And with several brisk steps he was outside.

The man's wife quickly filled in the silence. She took two plates and filled them with food before setting them before Kellie and the lieutenant. "Here, enjoy and eat as much as you wish." She said with a smile as she turned back to her seat at the table.

Within minutes their host returned. "Can't pass up the opportunity to dine with our soldiers! Haven't been able to do so in some time." He said with respect as he settled himself across from Kelley and the lieutenant. He proceeded to keep the two soldiers busy with questions about the war as they ate their food.

Towards the end of their meal, the lieutenant pushed back his plate, "My friend, thank you for your hospitality and for this meal. We won't stay for breakfast because we need to return to our command as soon as we can, so if you show us our place of sleep, we will retire."

"Oh, I can give you breakfast anyway. Here, I'll tell you where to sleep." Their host insisted as the three men stood.

Kelley proceeded to let his tired mind wander as he heard the man addressing the lieutenant, as he assumed they'd sleep in the same room. Suddenly, he snapped to attention when he realized he was now being spoken to. "Young man," their host was saying, looking at him. "You go upstairs, into the room with the open door."

Kelley nodded silently, too tired to ask for details, "Thank you sir," He said as he walked towards the staircase.

He slowly climbed the stairs, saw a room with an open door and a small candle burning inside on a table. He entered the room and saw the bed was in the far corner. As he approached it, he noticed there was someone in the bed. It was common for multiple soldiers or guests boarding in a home to sleep in the same bed, so Kelley took his shoes off, blew out the candle, and dropped into the bed. He rolled over to hit the man, to let him know he had company- but he didn't respond, so Kelley rolled back and quickly fell asleep.

Sometime during the night, Kelley jerked awake. There were voices speaking outside his room, then he heard someone ask, "Why, who put out the candle?" Somebody entered the room and re-lit the candle. Kelley, through cracked eyelids, saw a man and a woman enter the room and sit at the table, with the woman facing him. They began talking in low voices, with Kelley straining to catch their conversation. *They aren't talking about me. But do I ever wish they'd get out! Don't they have better manners, to let a soldier sleep!* He thought with frustration. He couldn't fall back asleep, so he quietly remained in bed, waiting for them to leave.

As he lay there several more minutes, the lady abruptly spoke, louder, to the man. "You ought to be ashamed of yourself to talk about such things in the presence of the dead."

In a split second, Kelley realized the man in bed besides him was dead. *He's dead! I don't intend on staying any longer!*

Without giving thought to his actions, he sat up and looked at the two at the table.

The lady noticed him first. With a scream that almost raised the roof off the home, she leapt up and sprinted out the room. The man turned to see what caused the scream, and seeing Kelley sitting up he yelled, leaped over the table, knocked it over, and scampered behind the lady out the room and down the stairs.

Kelley picked up his shoes and clothes besides the bed and hurried outside the room. The lady's scream scared the daylights out of him, and his ears were still ringing. He saw another room down the hall with its door open, so while holding his breath he scampered into that room. He shut the door and quickly rolled into bed while attempting to take deep, even breaths. He heard the commotion downstairs get louder. Soon, footsteps thundered up the stairs. He heard the lieutenant call, "Where's Kelley?" Eventually, the lieutenant began pounding on Kelley's door. "Kelley! Open up! Quick!"

Kelley slowly got out of bed and dragged his feet across the room, feigning exhaustion. "What now, I'm coming." He slowly opened the door and the lieutenant pushed himself into the room. He looked at Kelley in shock. "Why Kelley, the dead could be raised with the noise going on outside. Don't tell me you slept through it!"

Kelley rubbed his eyes and yawned. He walked to the bed and sat on it. "What?" He mumbled.

"Kelley!" The lieutenant plopped himself down on the edge of the bed. "They're saying a dead man in the other room came to life!"

Kelley looked at the lieutenant with his eyes half-shut. "Nonsense, leave me alone." And with that, he rolled back into the bed with his face away from the lieutenant.

The lieutenant shrugged and exited the room. He noticed the whole household was standing outside the dead man's door, afraid to go in. "Give me the candle." He commanded as he took a candle from a man standing there. "If he is not dead he needs attention." He boldly entered the room and noticed that the bed's sheet was rumpled. He bent forward to look at the man. "Why, the man is dead. The wind just blew the sheet off." He said as he pulled the sheet back over the body.

"No sir, that man rose and was sitting up looking at me!" The man who was in the room when Kelley sat up shakily exclaimed.

Meanwhile, Kelley lay in bed listening to the conversation in the other room. He could not fall back asleep, even as the commotion calmed down.

As dawn came and the roosters began to crow, he slipped out the house to the stables. He saddled up their horses, went back into the house to wake up the lieutenant, and before the rest of the house woke up both soldiers left.

"I still can't believe what happened last night." The lieutenant chuckled as he rode besides Kelley. "And you were too tired to care!"

Kelley glanced at the lieutenant, but didn't respond.

After riding for about twelve miles in silence, Kelley spoke up. "If I tell you something, promise to not tell anyone?"

"What is it?" The lieutenant asked, turning his head to look at Kelley.

"I was the reason everyone thought the man came to life yesterday."

"What do you mean?" The lieutenant stopped his horse.

"Well, I thought the room with the dead man was mine. I just thought he was another soldier boarding up for the night. During the night a man and a woman entered the room and woke me up with their voices, but I remained in bed. When I heard the woman mention the man beside me being dead, I wasn't goin' to stay in bed with him anymore! I sat up and they all thought the man came to life."

The lieutenant listened with a grin. By the end of the story, he was laughing uproariously. He slid off his horse's back and bent over, laughing and slapping his thighs. "You were the man who came to life!" He hollered as tears ran down his face. "You should have seen the man who saw you. He truly thought the dead came to life."

Kelley remained on his horse, looking at his lieutenant. "I guess it's funny. Come on, we need to get going." He urged. "Stop laughing."

The man laughed all the harder. Kelley's patience wore out. "I'm going without you." He said as he turned his horse back in the direction they were heading. "See you later."

After several miles of riding alone the lieutenant caught up with Kelley. Though nothing more was said about the incident, occasionally the lieutenant's sides would heave with silent laughter as he recalled the event. Even Kelley couldn't help smiling as he thought about the reaction of the man and woman.

When they returned to their command, the lieutenant didn't keep the event a secret. He related the incident to Kelley's general, who was also greatly amused.

No matter where I go, they want to hear the story. Kelley thought with amusement. *I just regret I never told my host who really sat up in that bed. Wonder if they still think the dead man came to life.*

Bonus Account

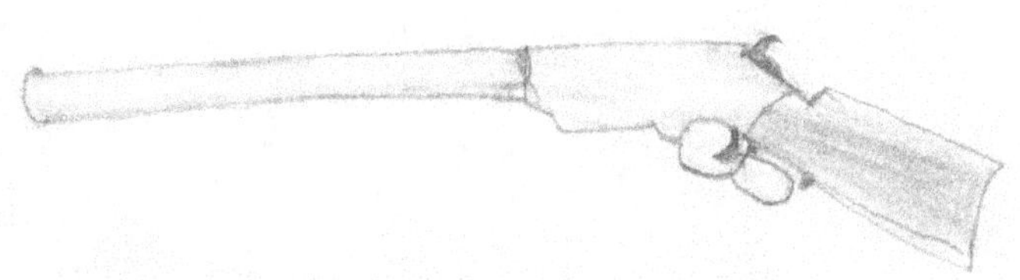

14. Greater Love Has No Man Than This

Union Commander John McNeil was exasperated. His headquarters were in Palmyra, Missouri, and two Missouri counties nearby had been torn apart by guerilla warfare between Union and Confederate sympathizers. McNeil recently ordered that a number of Confederates be jailed and held as hostages in exchange for the good behavior of their Confederate friends. Among those imprisoned was William Humphrey, a farmer and father of seven children.

***

William Humphrey sat in the crowded jail cell, amazed at the turn of events. He had been minding his own business and hoped his friends would behave themselves so he could return to his family. He heard voices outside the cell door, and heard a key turn in the lock. The heavy door swung open, and a middle-aged man entered the cell. All heads in the cell turned and looked expectantly at their visitor. "Men, I am Commander McNeil. You," He said, pointing to William and two other men, "Follow me."

The three prisoners looked at each other fearfully as they stood and followed McNeil out the cell to McNeil's personal office. McNeil sat down and motioned for the men to do the same. "Men, this jail is overcrowded. I am going to parole you. You may not leave this town, and if you sign and pledge your farms that you will keep the parole, you will be released from jail."

"Why, of course I will!" William said.

McNeil looked over at the others, who heartily echoed Williams' words.

"Yes sir please, where are those parole papers to sign?"

Upon signing the pledge and leaving prison, William was overjoyed. He went to a local inn and booked there for some time. He made sure to write to his family and let them know what was happening, and he waited for more news.

One morning, several weeks after his release upon parole, William was drinking his coffee at a table in the inn. He sighed and leaned back contentedly.

Suddenly, he heard a commotion outside the inn. The muffled words of "Fire!" were being shouted by the townspeople. William put his cup down and glanced out the window. People were frantically running by. He sprang from his seat and ran out the door.

"Where's the fire?" He asked.

"The jail!" A local who heard the question exclaimed.

William headed over to the jail. By the time he arrived, the jail had been evacuated and the fire put out. Smoke was still rising from the ashes.

Commander McNeil was outside the jail, and he was handing all prisoners a paper telling them they could return home but would have to report to the Federal headquarters regularly.

William walked up to McNeil. "Sir, does this mean I can return as well?" He hesitantly asked.

McNeil looked up from a paper he was signing. "Yes sir. However, you must report once a week at my headquarters. Here, take this document. You're as free as can be under the circumstances."

William reached out and took the paper. "Thank you sir!" He briskly walked to the inn, gathered his few belongings, and began the walk back to his town. The distance to his home was about ten miles, and the thought of seeing his family again made William nearly run all the way.

Here it is! The last bend in the road! He thought. He hurried around the bend. His little house appeared in sight, and he saw several of his children playing outside. His heart skipped a beat. "Molly! Betsey! Mark! John! Your daddy's home!" William shouted.

Startled, his kids looked up. His youngest, Molly, began running towards him. "Daddy! Daddy!"

The rest of his children recovered from the surprise and followed their sister, running to their father with outstretched arms.

The rest of the family heard the commotion and came out to see what was the matter. His wife ran out of the home to her husband, and hugged him over all their children hugging him.

"William! I never thought you'd return!" She said, her voice cracking.

He smiled. "Me neither Esther. There was a fire at the jail and all men were released. I do have to report back to the Federal headquarters once a week though.

Esther smiled. "No matter, you are home with us now." The family began to slowly walk towards their home. "But we missed you so much. We wanted to visit you while you were on parole, but our wagon wheel fell off after it got stuck in the mud and we had trouble putting it back on. I would have walked, but the little ones would have had some trouble." Esther said.

"I missed you too. I understand, you had double the work here on the farm without me. You should've told me about the wagon - I would've had someone come fix the wagon. Now that I'm back I'll get to work." William said.

***

One bright sunny morning several weeks after his return home, William prepared to head to town to report on his parole. He hugged his family goodbye and began to walk down the road. Upon arriving in town he headed to the Federal Headquarters, when a man in military uniform stopped him. "Halt, who are you?"

"Sir, I am William Humphrey and have come into town to report on my parole."

"We'll see about that. You're coming with me." The man said. He pulled handcuffs out of his pocket and walked towards William.

Shock covered William's face. "What did I do wrong?" He

cried.

"Nothing. I am William Strachan, the provost marshal." The man replied while snapping the cold handcuffs on William's wrists. He then led William down a flight of stairs to the basement, opened the door, took the handcuffs off, and shoved William in. The door slammed shut, and all was quiet.

William looked around the dark room. He made out the figures of several men- one looked vaguely familiar, as he looked like his neighbor. "Thomas?" He asked hesitantly.

"William! Oh, no, they got you too?"

"I reported on my parole and got thrown in here without explanation. What's going on?" William demanded, his mind still reeling over the event.

Thomas sighed, "A man who supported the Union recently disappeared- killed, we guess, by Southern sympathizers. McNeil ordered that if the men who killed this man or if the man himself was not turned up within five days, ten Confederate sympathizers would be shot. That's who we are."

William's face went pale. "What?" He asked incredulously.

Thomas nodded. "Tonight McNeil will send men out throughout the countryside to alert the people of what will happen. Your family will hear about it no doubt."

William shook his head and sank to the floor with his back against the cold wall. He placed his face in his palms. *Oh Esther, kids*, he thought. *What will you do without me?*

***

The next morning the town awoke to confusion and despair. Families and friends of the men to be killed were frantically entering the town. Among them was William's wife.

Esther and the kids came riding in their wagon. All the children were quiet and Esther was looking for the Federal building. Her son, James, was driving the wagon. "James, stop there." His mom said pointing to a larger office with a crowd of people gathered outside. "We're going inside. Follow me." She got out the wagon, took the youngest in her arms, and hurried up to the building with the rest of her children following.

Esther walked towards several Union soldiers guarding the front door. They stepped up as she approached with her kids. "Sirs, please let me in to talk to your commander." Esther pleaded.

The soldiers looked at each other hesitantly. "Ma'am we were ordered to not let anyone in...we are sorry but you cannot enter."

Esther desperately looked back at her children. "Please," She pleaded. "Your commander is going to kill an innocent man who has seven children."

One of the young soldiers glanced behind Esther at her kids, then looked at his comrades. He cleared his throat and spoke up, "Ma'am, I can try and see what we can do for you." He turned and entered the building.

"Thank you," Esther called after him. She stood by the door, wringing her hands and looking from the door to her children.

The crowd was pressing in, and the soldiers by the door were doing their best to keep the people from breaking into the Federal

Headquarters. "Stand back!" They cried.

After about five minutes the young soldier opened the door. Esther looked at him expectantly. He motioned for her to follow him. She gathered her skirts and quickly entered the building. "Ma'am, Commander McNeil said he will speak with you. If you will follow me." The soldier said.

"Oh, thank you so much sir!" Esther said as she briskly followed him, with her seven children close behind.

The soldier nodded but did not reply. Upon reaching the commander's office, he knocked and waited.

The door opened, and an older yet pleasant looking gentleman looked out. He smiled at Esther, "I have been told you would like to speak with me? Come on in." He led her in the room, nodded to the soldier, and shut the door.

He sat at his desk, and motioned for Esther to do the same. Her children sat on the floor and on other chairs scattered throughout the room. "Who are you? What would you like to say?" He kindly asked.

Esther began in a strained, trembling voice. "Sir, I am the wife of William Humphrey who you are holding hostage in the basement. Please, please do not kill my husband! Hasn't he dealt honorably with you? Didn't he keep his parole? He obeyed your orders, and suddenly when reporting for his parole he gets locked up again? Sir please do not go through with your threat. Do not leave William's seven young children fatherless!"

McNeil sat with his arms crossed during the whole speech. As

Esther ended there were several moments of silence before he spoke. "Ma'am, you are right. Mr. Humphrey kept his promises. And I cannot bear the thought of your children being fatherless- I have five young ones myself." McNeil stood and paced the room. "But justice needs to be served...a command is a command. Ma'am, children, wait here."

McNeil stood and left the room, leaving a confused Esther behind. Several minutes later McNeil opened the door, with William behind him. "William!" Esther leapt up and embraced him. Their kids all crowded around their father.

McNeil cleared his throat. "Stay here. I have an errand for Strachan, the provost marshal. He is to find a substitute for William." With that, McNeil quickly left the room and headed off to find Strachan. William and his family walked over to the window and looked out while waiting.

***

"Strachan!" McNeil called while approaching him. The marshall snapped to attention. "Strachan, you need to go find another man, a substitute for William Humphrey."

"Yes sir." The marshall replied. He walked outside to the courtyard. There, he noticed a young man preparing to leave, so Strachan approached him.

"What is your name?"

"Hiram Smith, sir." The twenty-one year old farmer replied, surprised.

"I have a warrant for you." Strachan said. He pulled out a blank death warrant and wrote Hiram Smith's name on it.

Hiram stood quietly. He looked up and noticed William and his entire family crowded around, looking out McNeil's office window. Hiram raised his eyebrows as if to ask, *Are you the man to be saved?* William barely nodded, unable to overcome a tightness in his throat.

Hiram turned and looked at Strachan. "It had better be me than that man with such a family." He said quietly.

Hiram followed the marshall across the courtyard to the prison. Before entering, Hiram stopped at a small well for a drink of water. "The way it is," he said matter of factly to the marshall as he filled a cup, "I can die as easily as drink that water." With that, he entered the prison.

McNeil entered his office shortly after. "William, family, we have found a substitute. However he would like to write some last letters and he doesn't know how to write. He asked that William help him. I'll bring him up to my office shortly, and you can help him."

William nodded. He turned to his wife. "Esther, take the children home. I will be back tomorrow." She silently gathered all the children and they filed out of the room, aware of the gravity of the situation.

Soon McNeil brought Hiram up to his office. "William, this is Hiram."

William reached out and shook Hiram's hand. He nodded, unable yet again to speak. McNeil gave William some paper and ink, and then left the room.

"Mr. Smith, I don't know what to say." William said before his voice broke off. "Thank you." He whispered.

Hiram leaned back in his chair and nodded. "Sir, I do not have a family. Only a wife. It would be better for me, a man without children, to die than you."

"But why are you doing this? You don't know me, yet you're willing to take my place. Why?" William asked. "And you seem to not be fearful of death. Why? I was tormented all this day thinking I was to be killed."

Hiram thought for a moment. "Why, I used to fear death too. I was tormented by the thought of what would happen to me after death. But now I know what'll happen to me and where I'll go after I die so I no longer fear death."

William leaned in. "I want the peace you have. What did you learn?"

Hiram smiled. "I know that I will go to heaven when I die. I used to think anyone who does good things can go to heaven, but that's not the case. I realized that I lied, stolen, dishonored my parents, hated others- and Jesus said whoever hates someone is a murderer. I had committed all these wrongdoings, and was therefore guilty before a perfect God."

"Well I've done all those bad things too but I still think I'll go to heaven." William said.

Hiram shook his head. "Try that in a court of law. You robbed a bank, killed a person, and then told the judge you deserve freedom, that you are not as bad as other people. Will he care? No. You'll still have to pay for your crimes. This is the same way with God. We stand imperfect, completely guilty before Him. We cannot just enter heaven like that. If you die the way you are in your sins you'll end up in hell."

"Well, is there hope?"

"Yes. Imagine you are in a courtroom again. You are faced with a fine of ten thousand dollars. You aren't able to pay that fine. But suddenly, someone walks into the courtroom and pays the judge ten thousand dollars. What happens? You gain your freedom. Jesus the Son of God did just this for us. Jesus came to earth, lived a perfect blameless life, and died on a cross in your place to pay for all the bad things, or sins, you committed. He stepped in your place, died in your place, and took the wrath of God upon Himself in your place. Because Jesus died on the cross and paid your fine, God can dismiss your case. All you need to do is to humbly repent of your sins and trust in Jesus alone. Repentance means to turn from your sins. And do not trust in your goodness to save you. Jesus said that our good works are like filthy rags before God. What you need to do is to turn from your sins, ask God to forgive you for your sins, and trust in Jesus to save you. I believe all this with my whole heart. I have repented from my sins, and because of that I no longer fear death." Hiram said.

William sat, stunned. He had never heard this before. To think he could have such peace in the face of death because he could know where he will spend eternity.

He looked out the window, pondering all he heard. Hiram sat silently, deep in thought as well.

To think Hiram will die in my place is unbelievable. It all makes sense now. Jesus died in my place...and Hiram will die in my place as well, so I can live.

William rubbed his forehead. "Hiram, it all makes sense. I don't know how I can live knowing you will die in my place- like Jesus did. I am a wretched man doomed for hell. Only Jesus can save me. I believe it all. Oh, but is there anything I can do for you?" he quietly asked.

Hiram smiled, "No, not for me. Please go talk to my wife tomorrow. She has heard about this situation. I was just with her before coming up here. Just please care for her if she ever needs any help. Go tell your family what I have told you. And one final thing, could I pray for you?"

William nodded, "Please, and..." he faltered "I want to pray too."

They bowed their heads and both men prayed. After ending Hiram looked up, "Now, about those letters I need to write." He said with a smile.

***

The next day William left the courthouse with determination. He couldn't remove the weight of what Hiram did for him. How a man could lay down his life for another still amazed and deeply sobered him. He began the walk to his home with a vision of what was ahead of him- to tell his friends and family of his new peace with God, and to make sure the legacy and story of Hiram lives on forever.

***

Several years later William and his wife had their eighth child, George. George grew up hearing the story of Hiram taking his father's place and was determined to honor the man who saved his father's life.

Once George got a job he arranged to have a monument built over Hiram's grave. The simple yet profound words are still on the monument to this day in Palmyra, Missouri:

THIS MONUMENT IS DEDICATED TO THE MEMORY

OF HIRAM SMITH

THE HERO THAT SLEEPS BENEATH

THE SOD HERE WHO WAS SHOT AT PALMYRA OCT 17,

1862

AS A SUBSTITUTE FOR WM T. HUMPHREY MY

FATHER.

G.W. HUMPHERY.

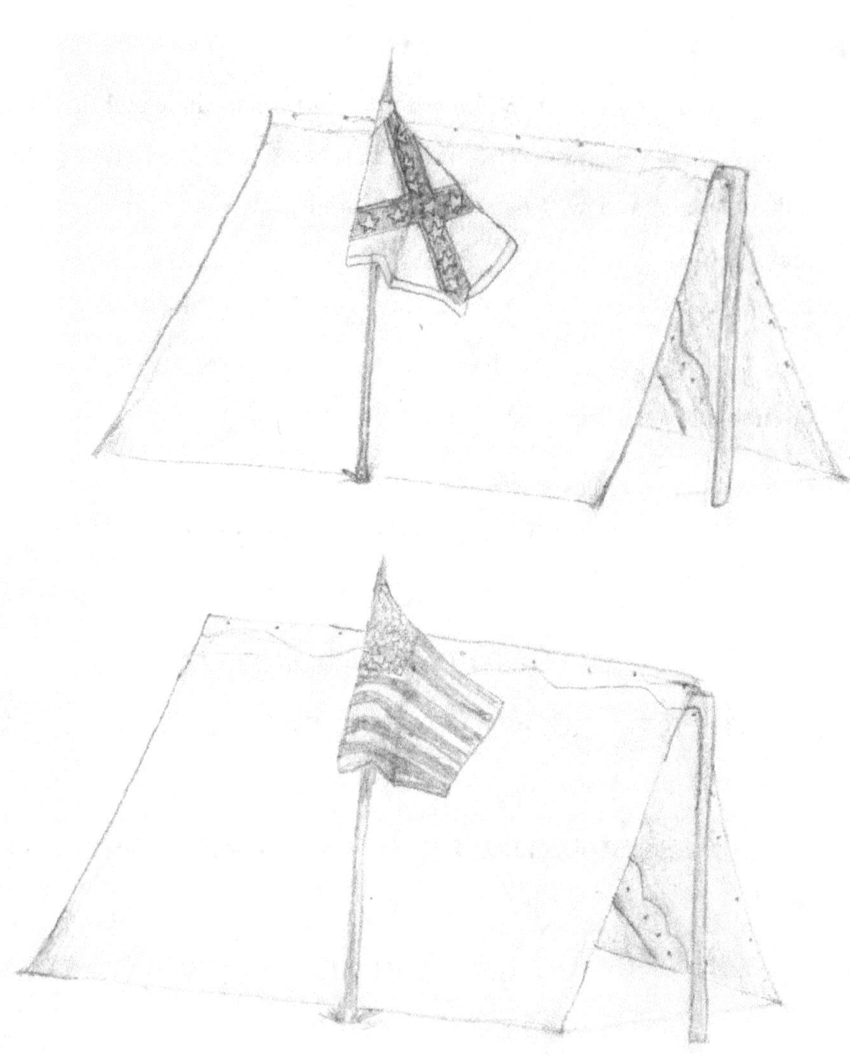